Just Clowning Around
Two Stories

Steven MacDonald
Illustrated by David McPhail

Green Light Readers
Harcourt, Inc.
San Diego   New York   London

Requests for permission to make copies of any part of the work should be mailed to:
Permissions Department, Harcourt, Inc., 6277 Sea Harbor Drive,
Orlando, Florida 32887-6777.

First Green Light Readers edition 2000
Green Light Readers is a registered trademark of Harcourt, Inc.

Library of Congress Cataloging-in-Publication Data
MacDonald, Steven (Steven K.)
Just clowning around/Steven MacDonald; illustrated by David McPhail.
—1st Green Light Readers ed.
p. cm.
"Green Light Readers."
Summary: A young bear and her dad, both circus clowns,
spend a day showing off their tricks for each other.
[1. Bears—Fiction. 2. Clowns—Fiction. 3. Tricks—Fiction.]
I. McPhail, David M., ill. II. Title.
PZ7.M478425Ju 2000
[E]—dc21 99-6798
ISBN 0-15-202512-X
ISBN 0-15-202518-9 (pb)

A C E G H F D B

A C E G H F D B (pb)

1
Clowning Around

Come on, Dad!

Dad, pass the dog!

Dad, pass the ham!

Dad, pass the cats!

See this, Dad?

Look at me, Dad!

Dad looks. And then . . .

Wow, Dad!

<u>2</u>
What Will Dad Do?

Dad is on his bike.

Watch out, Dad!

The bike tips. *Hisssss!*

What did Dad hit?

What will Dad do?

Tap, tap, tap.

Dad sits on his bike. *Hissssss!*

Now what will Dad do?

Meet the Illustrator

David McPhail clowns around when he paints pictures. He has fun creating stories about animals, such as the father and child bears in this story.

Many of David McPhail's books have bears in them. He likes to draw bears. They remind him of Teddy, the bear he had when he was a child. He and Teddy would clown around together.

Who do you clown around with?

David McPhail